Word Wise with Wordsworth

a picture is worth a thousand words—when a picture can describe something better than words can (idiom, page 12)

accept—to agree, receive, or approve of willingly (verb, page 29)

accomplish—to achieve or carry out (verb, page 27, *accomplished*)

assistance—the help given to another person (noun, page 24)

attract—to pull attention toward something or someone (verb, page 9)

bother—to worry or annoy (verb, page 8)

complete—finished or having all the parts (adjective, page 17)

demonstrate—to show or explain something to others (verb, page 7)

depart—to leave or go away (verb, page 19, *departed*)

depict—to describe or draw (verb, page 17, *depicted*)

examine—to look at something very carefully (verb, page 15, *examined*)

flourish—to prosper and thrive (verb, page 27)

impossible—not to be done or not likely to happen (adjective, page 14)

memorable—good enough to be worth remembering (adjective, page 18)

perplexed—puzzled or troubled by doubt (adjective, page 20)

remove—to take or do away with (verb, page 20, *removed*)

shabby—worn-out or tattered (adjective, page 22)

shocked—surprised or stunned (adjective, page 23)

spectacular—remarkable or impressive (adjective, page 11)

uncomfortable—not at ease or awkward (adjective, page 10)

vibrant—dazzling or radiant (adjective, page 12)

A Picture Is Worth A Thousand Words

by Quinn Alexander
Illustrated by Kelly Kennedy

SCHOLASTIC INC.

New York Toronto London Auckland Sydney
Mexico City New Delhi Hong Kong Buenos Aires

It was a big day for the kids in Mrs. Harris's second-grade class. For the last month, they'd been working in groups on a special project about the history of their town. Now they would finally get to **demonstrate** what they had learned. The class was celebrating Cloverhill Day, with student reports in the morning, a party at noon, and a special field trip later in the day.

Marco and Abby couldn't wait for the festivities to begin. They were very proud of all the research they had done for their oral report. And they were *really* happy with their visual aid: a 3-D map that showed what Cloverhill looked like in 1910. But they were also a little nervous, because Mrs. Harris had invited parents to come see the kids present their projects.

"Welcome, everyone. Welcome to Cloverhill Day," Mrs. Harris said, as the grownups began to arrive. "Please find a seat. We've set up some extra chairs, but you can also sit at the desks."

The students were standing at one side of the room, waiting to give their reports. Abby and Marco smiled and waved when their parents came in and sat down. But then Abby had to turn away. Her tall dad looked so funny squashed into a small chair, she was afraid she would get the giggles. So she looked at Wordsworth instead.

The cockatoo had been the class pet for longer than anyone could remember. Teachers had come and gone. Students had come and gone. But Wordsworth was always there—always cheerful and friendly and ready to repeat what Abby called "teacher talk." Everyone at Webster School loved him. No one except Abby and Marco knew his secret: that he took them on magical adventures to the Cloverhill of 100 years ago.

Today, there was a lot of commotion in the classroom, but it didn't **bother** Wordsworth. His crest was up, and he kept hopping around his cage to get a view of all the guests.

Abby nudged Marco. "Looks like Wordsworth is ready for the party," she said.

Marco nodded. "I just wish he could talk here, in the present, the way he does in the past," he said. "Then he could be part of our history report." Abby grinned. "Yeah, I can just picture it." She turned her head to one side and blinked at Marco. "Excellent reasoning. Very perceptive." she said, imitating Wordsworth's voice.

Mrs. Harris was trying to **attract** everyone's attention, without much success. Finally she clapped her hands. "One, two, three—all eyes on me!" she said.

"All eyes on me. All eyes on me," Wordsworth repeated, and everyone *did* look at him—and cracked up.

"Thank you, Wordsworth," said Mrs. Harris. "Now let's start our celebration."

Two by two, the students presented their reports, which covered many time periods in Cloverhill's history. Some students had made posters; some showed old photos. Two kids had created a 1925 version of the local newspaper, the *Cloverhill Times*. Two others in old-fashioned costumes acted out President McKinley's visit to town in 1887. Abby noticed that they kept tugging on their clothes, as if they were **uncomfortable**. She knew just how they felt!

Finally it was Abby and Marco's turn. Their 3-D map was on the worktable, covered with a sheet so that no one could see it until the right moment. When they lifted the sheet, everyone gasped.

The map was **spectacular**! The kids had used paints to create the farmland, the streets, and the two rivers: the Big Muddy and the Little Muddy. They had used small boxes, colored with markers, to make the buildings. And they had stuck on twigs and small plants to represent trees and bushes. They had even added Marco's model train and some tracks at the edge of town.

"In the early 1900s, Cloverhill looked very different from how it looks now," Abby began. She and Marco then went on to describe some of the buildings that were landmarks in Cloverhill 100 years ago. The other kids and the parents listened carefully. For them, this was all new. But for Marco and Abby, it was very familiar—not only because of the hours they had spent on the project, but also because they had actually visited the places they were talking about.

Everyone clapped loudly when they finished. Marco and Abby grinned. They had done what they had set out to do, and their project was a success.

The rest of the kids gave their reports. Then there was a party with sandwiches, veggies and dip, fruit salad, and a special cake from Aunt Franny's bakery. After the parents left, Mrs. Harris and the class set off on their field trip: a visit to town hall. Their tour guide turned out to be none other than Mrs. Novak, the mayor of Cloverhill.

Mayor Novak welcomed the class and told them a little bit about her job. Then she led them into a large room with many seats. "This is my favorite room in the building," she said. "Isn't it beautiful? It's the hall where the town council meets."

Marco and Abby looked around. The hall had tall, white pillars and a high ceiling painted in **vibrant** colors. But it was the huge paintings on the walls that made the room special. There were six of them, and they were full of amazing detail.

"Take your time looking at the murals," said the mayor. "They were created by a local artist who went on to become very famous, and each one shows an important moment in Cloverhill's history." She paused and smiled at the kids. "Now, I'm a big fan of reading. But in this case, I think **a picture is worth a thousand words**. Seeing these murals is seeing history come alive."

"Can you tell us the artist's name?" asked Mrs. Harris.

"Oh, didn't I say?" replied Mayor Novak. "It's André Durand."

Abby almost fell over in surprise. André Durand was the artist whose house had nearly burned in the fire the last time they had visited Cloverhill.

"We met him! Marco and I met him," she blurted out. Then she realized what she had done and slapped a hand over her mouth.

"I'm afraid that's **impossible**, dear," said Mayor Novak. "The murals were painted in the 1920s."

"Sorry, I made a mistake," Abby said.

Quickly, she turned and pretended to study the nearest mural. Marco had turned with her. "I can't believe I did that," she whispered to him.

"The only mistake you made was telling the mayor," he said softly. "We *did* meet André Durand, and this painting proves it."

For the first time, Abby carefully **examined** the mural. It was a nighttime view of Cloverhill. The artist had painted the night of the first-ever Cloverhill Town Fair. It was a wonderful, happy scene—until you noticed that a shed was on fire, and flames were spreading across a field toward a cluster of houses.

"It's the night we were there—the night of the fire!" exclaimed Abby in amazement.

"That's right," said Marco. "Now look at the church."

Abby looked. The door to the church tower was open; and inside, pulling on the bell rope to raise the alarm, were two kids: a red-haired girl and a dark-haired boy. A large white bird flew above the church.

Abby's eyes lit up. "That's us, Marco!" she whispered. "That's us—and Wordsworth."

The rest of the field trip went by in a blur. Abby and Marco were so amazed at finding themselves **depicted** in the mural, they couldn't take in anything else the mayor said. Luckily, no one noticed. By the time the class returned to school, all the kids were tired. So Mrs. Harris read aloud to them for the last half hour.

Finally the school day was over. Mrs. Harris stood at the door, saying good-bye, as her students left the room. But Abby and Marco stayed behind to clean up the worktable, put away art supplies, and gather up the books they had borrowed from the library.

Marco took the special map of Cloverhill from his desk. When they had first found it tucked into an old history book, it had been blank in spots. But after each of their visits to the past, a building had magically appeared. Now the map looked much more **complete**.

"What should we do with this?" he asked Abby. "I guess we should return it to the library, along with the book, but . . ."

"But we don't really want to," Abby finished. "I think we should hold on to it, and see what else shows up when we visit the past. We can always return it later."

Mrs. Harris came back into the room. "What a wonderful, **memorable** day," she said. "But I could use a cup of coffee. If you don't mind, I'll zip down to the teachers' room and get one. Then I'll help you put everything away."

"That would be great, Mrs. Harris," said Marco.

"Take your time," said Abby.

As soon as she **departed**, they hurried over to Wordsworth's cage. Usually, the minute she was out of sight, he would say, "Open the door," and they would be off on a new adventure. But he just sat on his perch and said nothing. In fact, he seemed to be asleep.

"Come on, Wordsworth," said Marco. "It's time to go."

"Say, 'Open the door,'" Abby said, imitating the bird's voice. Wordsworth still said nothing.

The kids kept begging him to say the magic words. Finally, Abby opened the door and **removed** him from the cage. But when she tried to get him to fly to Mr. Keys's room, he clung to her arm. That's when Mrs. Harris returned with her coffee.

"Is something wrong?" she asked. "Is Wordsworth sick?"

"He's fine," Marco said quickly. "We were just going to take him to see Mr. Keys."

Mrs. Harris looked **perplexed**. "I guess that's OK. But if Mr. Keys is busy, come right back."

Abby and Marco hurried down the hall. The custodian was at his desk, not really doing anything. "Hello," he said. "I thought you might stop by this afternoon."

The kids barely slowed down. "*Um,* we need to get something from the supply shelves," Abby said, and they hurried to the back of the room.

Nothing happened. The shelves did not melt away. The tunnel to the past did not appear. There was no loud pop or flash of light.

Mr. Keys joined them. "I'm sorry, kids," he said gently. "The door is closed. Your adventures are over—at least for now."

"No! It can't be closed," cried Marco.

"That's not fair!" said Abby.

Then it hit them: Mr. Keys knew about their visits to the past.

"Come and sit down. We have a lot to talk about," he said, leading them back to his desk. He took Wordsworth from Abby and settled him on the arm of his chair. Then he pulled over a couple of **shabby** old chairs for the kids, and they all sat down.

Marco and Abby were silent, their minds spinning.

"How . . . how did you know?" Marco finally asked.

"Because I did the same thing," said Mr. Keys.

Now the kids were doubly **shocked**. Their jaws dropped, and their eyes opened wide.

"Let me explain," said Mr. Keys. "About 20 years ago, I was a second grader at Webster Elementary. Mrs. Harris wasn't my teacher, but Wordsworth was the class pet. One day he showed me the secret passageway to the past—the same way he did for you."

"You mean, you traveled to Cloverhill in the early 1900s, too?" asked Abby.

"No," said Mr. Keys. "I went back to the 1850s."

Marco leaned over to stroke Wordsworth's head. "That explains something I always wondered about," he said. "The second time we visited the past, Wordsworth told us he had made the trip many times. He must have meant with you."

"Maybe, maybe not," said Mr. Keys. "Wordsworth has been around for years. Who knows how many times he's said, 'Open the door.' When I took the custodian's job here, I figured someone else might get the chance to time-travel. When I saw it was you, I made sure to stay close by in case you needed **assistance**."

"But we didn't," Marco said proudly.

Mr. Keys nodded. "I was right when I said, 'You're smart, you'll figure it out.' Because you did!"

Abby grinned. "Here's one of the things that we figured out: we played baseball with your great grandfather."

It was Mr. Keys's turn to be surprised. "You're kidding! You played with Theodore Alexander?"

"That's right," said Marco, "only he told us his name was Ted."

"Ted was his nickname. He was second in what's turned out to be a long line of Theodores," said Mr. Keys. "His son was called Theo, and Theo's son was called Teddy, and then there's me."

"But you're Mr. Keys," said Abby.

"That's just what everyone at school calls me—because of these." He jingled the big ring of keys on his belt. "But my real name is Theodore Alexander, and I'm the fifth one. So my nickname is Quinn—which means five. Quinn Alexander."

"Cool," said Marco.

Mr. Keys asked the kids to tell him about their adventures. So they described some of the exciting things they had done.

When they were through, Mr. Keys nodded. "Here's what I think," he said. "Somehow Wordsworth senses when Cloverhill is at a turning point, when it could either **flourish** and grow, or it could die out—the way lots of little towns have. He knows where the doorways between the past and present are hidden, and he's the key that opens them. But he's a bird. He can't do anything on his own. So he finds kids to help."

"Like you and me and Marco," put in Abby.

"That's right," said Mr. Keys. "You two figured out what needed to be done and you did it, and that's why Cloverhill is the great place it is today. Think about everything you **accomplished**. Better yet, make a list." He handed Abby a pad and pencil.

1. Got Mr. Webster to donate land for the school.
2. Found a new doctor for Cloverhill.
3. Saved the *Cloverhill Times* from going out of business when it was robbed.
4. Gave the Hamiltons the idea to turn their house into a library.
5. Helped Ted and other kids start Buster Blaze Field.
6. Convinced Aunt Franny to start her bakery.
7. Saved Mr. Ward, who helped build the bridge over the Big Muddy.
8. Caught the fake ghost who was making the Maplewood Inn lose guests.
9. Helped Mr. Gilmore start his business.
10. Gave the mayor the idea for the Cloverhill Town Fair.
11. Saved the town from a fire.

When they were done, Marco gave Mr. Keys the list. "Wow! This is impressive," he said. "Good work, you guys."

"Good work! Good work!" echoed Wordsworth.

Marco and Abby smiled sadly. They both felt very proud of what they had done. But at the same time, it was hard to **accept** that their adventures were over.

Marco stood up. "We had better go," he said. "Mrs. Harris is waiting, and we have to clean up our stuff."

Mr. Keys put Wordsworth back on Abby's arm. "Come visit me anytime. I would love to tell you about what happened when *I* visited the past," he said.

"That would be great," said Marco. He started to leave, but Abby paused a moment.

"Mr. Keys, do you think we'll ever get to go back?" she asked.

"We can always hope," he said. "Who knows? The door may open again someday."

Get Your Word's Worth

After you finish reading this book together, use the prompts below to spark thoughtful conversation and lively interaction with your child.

- ♣ Marco and Abby both hope that they can have more trips with Wordsworth in the future. Do you think their time traveling is **complete**, or will they return one day to the Cloverhill of 100 years ago? Why?

- ♣ With their 3-D map, Marco and Abby **demonstrated** to the class how the town of Cloverhill had changed over time. If you made a map of your town, what buildings would you include?

- ♣ Marco and Abby were **shocked** to discover that Mr. Keys knew their secret. What parts of Cloverhill do you think Mr. Keys visited during his adventures into the past?